Poems from a Witch's Pocket

Laura Theis

ILLUSTRATED BY
KATE LUCY FOSTER

*for all the magic-weavers
with secrets in their pockets*

THE EMMA PRESS

First published in the UK in 2025 by The Emma Press Ltd.

Poems © Laura Theis 2025.

Illustrations © Kate Lucy Foster 2025.

All rights reserved.

The right of Laura Theis and Kate Lucy Foster to be identified as the creators of this work has been asserted in accordance with the Copyright, Designs and Patents Act 1988.

ISBN 978-1-915628-42-8

A CIP catalogue record of this book is available from the British Library.

Printed and bound by CMP Digital Print Solutions, Poole.
Edited and typeset by Emma Dai'an Wright.

**EU GPSR Authorised Representative
LOGOS EUROPE,** 9 rue Nicolas Poussin,
17000, LA ROCHELLE, France
E-mail: Contact@logoseurope.eu

The Emma Press
theemmapress.com
hello@theemmapress.com
Jewellery Quarter,
Birmingham, UK

PRAISE FOR POEMS FROM A WITCH'S POCKET

'A mix of tenderness and teeth, *Poems from a Witch's Pocket* is a book of spells, incantations, wisdom and fun, perfect for sharing or keeping all to yourself.' Kiran Millwood Hargrave

'It manages to delight and provoke; it is playful and moving but never fey (which is harder than it sounds). There is depth and complexity here – about ecology, about friendship – but this is all worn lightly and the tone is sustained with great skill and beauty from start to finish.'
Kate Wakeling, Judge of the Caterpillar Prize 2025, on 'I complain to my friend who has been turned into a tree'

OTHER TITLES AVAILABLE FROM THE EMMA PRESS

POETRY COLLECTIONS FOR CHILDREN

Eggenwise, by Andrea Davidson, illus. by Amy Louise Evans
Balam and Lluvia's House, by Julio Serrano Echeverría, tr. from Spanish by Lawrence Schimel, illus. by Yolanda Mosquera
Cloud Soup, by Kate Wakeling, illustrated by Elīna Brasliņa
My Sneezes Are Perfect, by Rakhshan Rizwan with Yusuf Samee, illustrated by Benjamin Phillips

THEMED POETRY ANTHOLOGIES FOR CHILDREN

The Bee Is Not Afraid of Me: A Book of Insect Poems
Dragons of the Prime: Poems about Dinosaurs
The Head that Wears a Crown: Poems about Kings and Queens
Watcher of the Skies: Poems about Space and Aliens
Falling Out of the Sky: Poems about Myths and Monsters

CHAPTER BOOKS & SHORT STORIES FOR CHILDREN

Please Don't Read the Footnotes Please, by Rob Walton
The Skeleton in the Cupboard, and other stories, by Lilija Berzinska, tr. from Latvian by Žanete Vēvere Pasqualini and Sara Smith
Na Willa and the House in the Alley, by Reda Gaudiamo, translated from Indonesian by Ikhda Ayuning Maharsi Degoul and Kate Wakeling, illustrated by Cecillia Hidayat

NOVELS FOR CHILDREN

The Untameables, by Clare Pollard, illus. by Reena Makwana
Oskar and the Things, by Andrus Kivirähk, illustrated by Anne Pikkov, translated from Estonian by Adam Cullen

SHORT STORIES AND ESSAYS

Bound: A Memoir of Making and Remaking, by Maddie Ballard
How Kyoto Breaks Your Heart, by Florentyna Leow
Night-time Stories, edited by Yen-Yen-Lu
Tiny Moons: A year of eating in Shanghai, by Nina Mingya Powles

POCKET CONTENTS

so you want to become a hovel witch 1
Menagerie 4
Note Found Next To An Empty Basket 5
wolf song 7
Five Clues For Working Out Which Bird You've Become 9
I complain to my friend who has been turned into a tree 13
A Poem In Which I Disagree With One Of My Favourites 15
how to walk on water 17
witches also have bad days 18
cave 20
Summoning Spell 21
where I travel at night 24
Disappointing Ducks 26
gift note 28
sapling 31
my sister dreams she is a garden 33
next time the sadness comes 34
October Cauldron Song 37
Party Planning Notes – Pumpkin Party – To Do 38

winter spell	40
B/AD	42
Refusal	45
Come In & Meet The Cat	47
Unfortunately The Witches' Code	49
the faraway siblings	51
Hibernation Spell	52
bad fairytale	53
Spell Song For Extra Courage	57
the solitude of guarding a dragon	58
Write your own poems!	63
Acknowledgements	67
Thank-yous	68
About the author	70
About the illustrator	71
About The Emma Press	72
Also from The Emma Press	73

so you want to become a hovel witch

to be a hovel witch
you need a cake tin full of nos

a few choice yeses stored out of sight
      you have to let the owls in

when they come knocking
let the small ones nest in your hair

the big ones on top of your wardrobe
      you must ignore the hairballs

they cough up   trust that somebody
will get rid them if they really mind

you need friends with strong stomachs
and a tolerance for difficult creatures

kind deaf neighbours
with a passion for baking

you have to work on
your perfect scream

acquire a good cackle that dances
the line between infectious and alarming

you'll need a hat and a blanket   jam jars and a pot
plus a healthy distrust of mirrors

you don't need a broom because let's face it
no one could suspect you of overly frequent sweeping

and there are more convenient ways to travel
    you need one book of spells and a library card

more sense than you were given
a broad view on humour

some trust in yourself
or imagination

you certainly don't need me
to tell you all this

because the wildest part of you
already chose

Menagerie

I carry a small menagerie
in my pocket:

Labradorite. Wulfenite.
Mookaite Jasper. Tiger Iron.

I marvel at their stony wildness,
pet their smooth round heads.

Note Found Next To An Empty Basket

Dear Neighbours,

Please do take as many as you like,
for I simply have too many

and the scaly little red one is almost ready to hatch!
Remember: dragon eggs don't shatter easily

but the more you sit on them the crosser
the hatchling when it gets out.

To incubate, I recommend instead
wrapping in leaves soaked with rainwater

and keeping in a swamp or, that not being possible,
in a constant fire for 999 days.

Good luck and thank you
for taking them off my hands!

W.

wolf song

wolves at our front door
& wolves by the back gate
they stalk through the foxgloves
like lost thoughts
they wait –
& they wait –
wait –
& they wail & they howl & they sing
but did they come here to kill us?
or to delight and to thrill us?
well my dear
wolf song's a coin toss
(like all magical things…)

Five Clues For Working Out Which Bird You've Become

If no bird baths present you
with a mirroring surface, don't fret:
there are countless ways to find out
what you are:

If you feel constantly sleepy, if you
answer every question with an ominous 'u-hu'
and everyone treats you like a dangerous queen,
you may have become an eagle owl…

If you find yourself overcome with echolalia,
unable to finish a conversation without repeating
what has just been said, you can be quite sure
you're a mockingbird, parrot or myna…

If you find yourself attracted to gold buttons
and eyeballs, you could be a corvid – most likely
a magpie if you begin riding the backs of deer
or strutting in slow, self-absorbed steps…

If you want to drape yourself heavy
around the neck of a lost soul
you might be an albatross – or a swan if you do it
while reciting the saddest song you've ever known…

But only as a starling will you gather
with thousands of strangers at dusk
and use your peerless polka-dot wings to write
an ever-changing poem for the sky.

I complain to my friend who has been turned into a tree

I complain to my friend
who has been turned into a tree:

You have it so easy.
She greens at me, wistfully.

Do I? She shakes her branches,
sways towards me. *What makes you think so?*

I just envy you, I say.
You're going to live

for hundreds of years,
with no stress, nothing to worry about.

She drops a leaf on me
as if I'm being stupid.

Not in this city I won't, not in this day and age.
I might even die before you. And as for stress,

how about winter, and water — too much of it
or too little, and what about soil compaction,

pollution, bug infestations, lice, exposure to road salt,
the construction site right by my roots?

What about fires and lightning? Sometimes the dust
on my leaves gets so thick I can no longer breathe.

You know those nightmares where you're rooted
to one spot and can't get away? I don't sleep now, not ever.

I fling my arms around her, feeling contrite.
Forgive me, I had no idea, I whisper into her bark.

You never asked.

A Poem In Which I Disagree With One Of My Favourites

'certainty is beautiful, but uncertainty is more beautiful still' – Wisława Szymborska

I really wish I could love
the uncertainty of change

or at least be less afraid of it

If only I knew a spell
to turn it softer

so we could wrap it around our shoulders
like a shawl of ever-changing colours

and feel a little bit
safe

*how to walk on water**

try turning yourself into
a fishing spider, pygmy gecko or basilisk

failing that, run across the shallows' surface
at twice the speed the water flows

or do it slowly, gingerly, on tiptoes
while holding a willow wand

(*best to practise on bath days
in the unlikely event that none of these work…)

witches also have bad days

let's say you're feeling uninspired
let's say that for days you haven't looked or
   been looked at by anyone

but the bird pattern of your duvet cover
and the backs of your own eyelids

did you know you can still make a spell song
from oxygen and the muscles you've been
   using for your long yawns?

that you can still turn a pebble into a grain of sand
and back again with a flick of your tired mind?

that you can fast forward or slow down time
as you are waiting to be let in, or for the good part
   to begin?

cave

when I needed to disappear
the ground made space for me

the weathered rock opened
like a mouth weighing a secret

and I understood it
would probably keep me

until I started waiting
for my self to arrive

like a knight back into
my own life

at which point it
would spell me out

to the world like a wish
to a fountain

Summoning Spell

Under a waning moon, send a familiar to gather:

> the shadow of a midnight fox
> eleven drops of daybreak
> caught in seven different cobwebs
> (with apologies for disturbing the spiders)
> the essence of a chimaera's sigh
> (though a disgruntled cow's will do in a pinch)

Add the creak of a door that opens by itself.

Stir well.

Wait.

Then, on one of the year's greyest days,
when fog nibbles at the edges of everything,
observe when a shadow moves through your thoughts.

Hold the potion aloft
and say:

> 'From the depths of night
> and the shades of day
> bring me a joy
> that isn't afraid'

(Then, when they arrive,
make sure to offer them a cup
of your darkest brew —)

where I travel at night

I don't need to bring a toothbrush
but I do need to know

what to say to a five-year-old squirrel boy
who is too smart for his own good

I need to know if I'm too heavy
for the mare I've been given

how to stake somebody's name
how to stay turned towards the light

I cannot take pictures here
I cannot write postcards

I cannot smuggle anything
back home

I'm allowed almost no memories
no travel companions

so why do I still return?
If I don't I will suffer, suffocate

I would misplace myself

Disappointing Ducks

Someone who almost never lies told me
one of the most important skills to master
is how to disappoint,

that one day it may save me
from living inside
someone else's script.

So today I will practice.
I'm starting with
the ducks.

They come at me with their sweet expectant waddle,
demanding bread
in soft but certain voices.

And I say, I'm sorry, I've nothing to offer today.
The ducks nod, seriously.
After short deliberation they decide

to keep me company regardless,
allowing me to watch their watery adventures
for nothing in return.

gift note

dear friend watch out / for these ghosts I raised
I admit I am out / of my depth

I know this will come as no surprise / to you
my whole life has primed me / to put myself in situations

where I don't know what on earth / I'm supposed to be doing
and do it regardless / see what happens

but anyway these ghosts / you see
they are very fragile / wispy little things

none of them have / good recall
even the dogs listen less / than in real life

in fact it turns out / there's no commanding
   them at all
it's like they can't hear you / but I hope you
   will like

their haunting and hovering and staring /
   they are so sorrowful and confused
a bit like us / a bit like the moon

be gentle with them / happy birthday

sapling

this sprouting acorn is a little ragamuffin
who's never been to nursery

she's never met her mother
she raised herself in bitter rain-soaked earth

but one day she'll grow up to be
an illustrious oak of renown

she will show them all
she will outgrow them all

my sister dreams she is a garden

my sister dreams she is a garden and as I run barefoot
down her winding paths I know not to step on the
  sharp stones
and where her early snowdrops grow

my sister dreams she is a garden and I am a snail
out in her dew until the sun burns the moisture away
so I must burrow deeper in order to stay

my sister dreams she is a garden and
I'm the trunk of a birch tree that's losing its leaves
and I'm its bare branches and I am its grief

my sister dreams she is a garden and I am a story
beloved by the snow I am what is lost to the silence
all that is covered and hidden below

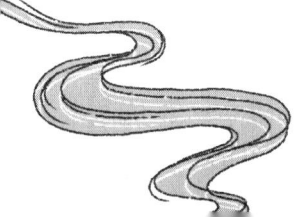

next time the sadness comes

a stranger will hand you
an unexpected rose

and vanish before you can
wonder if you need to

force your face into a brave shape
as you stand there and hold it close

that sweet scent on a thorn stick
a true smile will break you

open: slow at first
then wide as a garden

you will understand this gift
as a bond between you and the places

where hope grows
you'll decide to save every petal

press them between the pages
of stories your future will write

October Cauldron Song

season of socks and scarlet dusk
season of ghost, apple and yearning
season of woodfire, wind and witch ash
season of burning, sleeping, turning
season of bramble dark and russet
season of crisp and creeping chill
season of gloves and wishful candles
season of gold and falling still
season of forest fox and waiting
season of harvest, spice and grain
season of scarf and mud and singing
season of hearth and smoke and rain

Party Planning Notes – Pumpkin Party – To Do

- Find pumpkin seed in pantry
(Careful not to confuse with dead bug look-alike again!)

- Try out rapid growing hex until pumpkin is about bat size
(If it doesn't work, timehop back to when you should have planted it in the first place, plant, water, timehop back.)

- Harvest pumpkin

- Quick nap

- Try out duplication charm (13x)

Make 12 bat-sized pumpkins to serve pumpkin soup in
& 1 cat-sized pumpkin to serve pumpkin juice in

- Maybe some extra ones to use as lanterns??

- Keep at least one seed for next year, make pumpkin-seed bread from the rest

- Ask neighbours to bring pumpkin pie

- Ask neighbours to bring extra pumpkins just in case!!!

winter spell

please frosten the grapes
for my winter cauldron

give me no more than
the sway of an ice wind

the dark heart of a twilight swan

give me no spring to believe in
just a fire to sit by

a snow storm to keep me
& endless night

a new moon

B/AD

*Stuck for a present
for your worst enemy?*

*Look no further than Handwritten Hexes,
putting the curse back in cursive since 1999!*

*From lost keys to wardrobe malfunctions,
no job is too small.
Turn calm pets into hellbeasts
or place a permanent pebble
in your opponent's shoe.*

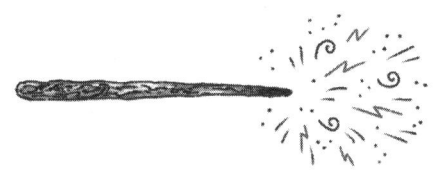

*Waiting to inherit a fortune?
Try our premium package:
trim a year or two off your
overly sprightly relative's life!*

*We're a family-run business
and use only recycled paper
and organic, locally-sourced
blood-ink!*

Refusal

To be perfectly honest,
in recent years I have grown quite fond
of the indoors.
How it keeps the weather out,
for one thing. Camping in the damp
of a deathly forest sounds
terrific of course, but I think there is
something to be said for a dry bed,
with no creepy crawlies or snakes.

You know what else I love
about staying put?
I mean, you name it.
The soft chairs? The life expectancy?
Floating around in my giant bath?
The only beasts one encounters here
are either served roasted at feasts
or chained up outdoors
to keep us safe from intruders.

Might that prophecy have been meant for
someone else with a similar name
in a neighbouring kingdom?
Just a funny coincidence I'm sure.
So really, while I appreciate your efforts
in reaching out, I'm good here.
No, really. Best of luck. Bye.

Come In & Meet The Cat

There used to be a cat
in this poem.

I swear.
I didn't take it out!

It was such a good cat too... a little thing of feral
beauty, sharp-clawed and mischievous...

but I must have left the window open
somewhere around the fourth stanza.

Or maybe I didn't close the door firmly enough
on the final line?

Either way, as you can see,
all that's left now

is the scratched-up sofa,
a relieved-looking goldfish

and some hairballs on the floor.

I'm embarrassed

I lured you here
with false promises.

I'm sorry to offer hairballs
when you were quite reasonably expecting

an actual cat. I guess we could wait a bit,
see if it comes back?

But no, this is already the antepenultimate line,
and the cat is still somewhere out there living
the best of its seven lives…

Unfortunately The Witches' Code

s

o

m

e

times

another witch

will waltz up to you

and poignantly make a point

of pointing out she has a pointier hat

the pointiest of hats in fact as if you weren't

the one who taught her that spell which lets you layer

sharp thread upon sharper thread like an ancient architect

(it might be tempting to accidentally conjure an elephant to accidentally sit on it for a bit until the hat is creased and crushed and crumpled button-flat, but unfortunately the witches' code *strictly* forbids you from doing that…)

the faraway siblings

I was born under a new moon and so
in my first few days of life
we grew alongside each other
my pale faraway sister and I

she taught me the importance of darkness
how to call the ocean close
how to reveal myself in increments
yet dream in a language of shadows

many dozens of moons orbits later
we find ourselves in sync again
just as on the day we first started
to push ourselves towards the brink again

Hibernation Spell

I summon first of all
a large round cloud of a bed

smelling of cocoa and snow drift
I summon a soft light

I invite the quiet
and banish the dread

I am only here to dream
I am only here to rest

bad fairytale

once upon a time
we didn't need
stories

there were no princesses
the third and youngest brother always did
exactly the same as the first two

animals never spoke and if they did
you could ignore
whatever they said

red riding hood wore
a midnight blue duffel coat
the wolf was very small
and good

grandmas were youthful and rich
the forest was safe and well lit
woodcutters retrained as estate agents

rapunzel had a pixie cut
her parents were still around
she lived in a nice bungalow

queens lived in hotels
some kings lived in hovels
castles were for the general public

everyone thought their step-mum
was the loveliest
(cinderella and snow white especially)

magic had no price attached whatsoever
there was no shoe-based torture, no anti-witch propaganda
so no children ever burned any in ovens

wishing didn't do anything
there was no kissing
nobody got married

no one got cursed
nothing much happened
and they all died at various points, disgruntled

Spell Song For Extra Courage

In thorny woods where darkness sleeps
I walk the path with shadowed feet.

Above, my sister lights the way
till night becomes a yawning day.

I won't turn back, won't doubt, won't fear.
I am a witch. My magic's here.

the solitude of guarding a dragon

no one told me
there's no greater solitude
than in guarding a dragon

day in and day out
this is surprising to me
after all the dragon is always right there

with its amber eyes and great heat
its music of ancient times
it's just the people that find themselves obliged

to stay away – the friends forced
to shout from faraway hilltops
out of range of the dragon's fire

it's just the parties I've
unwittingly uninvited myself from by
linking my lot to a giant reptile

of breathtaking beauty and unpredictable moods
this covetous monster which never sleeps
I can tell myself this is what I chose

hang baubles from its tusks at christmas
paint eggs on its scales for easter
brush its teeth for fireworks at new year

I can ride it at night and
find fellowship in the way
the stars overhead never stop moving

as if they don't dare
let their guard down either
and I can cheer myself up

with tales of heroes
those legends in our stories and songs
who'd willingly risk a bit of dragon fire

for nothing
but the pleasure
of my company

WRITE YOUR OWN WITCHY POEMS!

To get you started, here are some ideas from editor Emma Dai'an Wright:

✹ In 'Note Found Next To An Empty Basket' (page 5) we get some handy instructions on how to look after dragon eggs, which I expect you could have worked out for yourself if you thought hard enough. What about pegasus eggs, though? Or a bunch of baby basilisks? Pick a mythical creature, consider their particular qualities,* and write a list of care instructions for them, for your neighbours or perhaps a friend who is egg-sitting for you.

✹ It happens to the best of us: you got on the wrong side of a sorcerer and they've turned you into a bird. Decide what kind of bird you've become (see page 9) and write a poem about it. You might need to do

---

* Do they breathe fire? Do they fly? Are they part-horse? Part-snake?

some research – where does this bird live? What does it eat? How does it behave? You could even include some backstory – how did you anger the sorcerer? How will you turn yourself back?

✳ Imagine everything that trees see in their long lifetimes! Weather, animals, people, other plants and buildings all around them – not to mention all the creatures that make their homes within them. We could all learn a lot from trees. In the poem on page 13, the witch has a chat with her friend who has been turned into a tree. Pick your own tree to talk to: maybe one you walk past every day, or one you see often. Write down what you would say to it, and then how the tree might reply, and turn these into a conversation poem, alternating between your comments/questions and the tree's responses.

✳ Even witches have bad days, as the poem on page 18 shows! If you're having a bad day, sometimes it can help to remind yourself of all your special qualities and magic powers. Write down a list of things that you can do, big or small. Then turn that list into a poem by starting each line with 'I can'. (You could include a mix of very real things about yourself and some possibly-more-fantastical ones – though who is to say what is true or not?)

✸ Write a thank-you note to your witch friend, who so thoughtfully sent you a set of ghosts for your birthday (page 28). How did you feel when you opened the package? Are the ghosts getting on with any creatures or people you might live with? What do they do all day?

✸ Do you have a favourite month of the year? What makes this month so special? Drawing on all your senses, jot down everything that you associate with this time of year: sights, smells, sounds, textures and tastes. Then use this list to write your own month poem in the style of 'October Cauldron Song' on page 37.

✸ The poem on page 57 is a spell to give extra courage. Can you think of anyone who is facing a difficult moment or situation, who needs to be especially brave right now? Using the second person ('you'), write an encouraging spell song for them, in the style of Laura's:

You won't turn back, won't doubt, won't fear.
You are a witch. Your magic's here.

In your first two lines, set the context: where is the person you are imagining? What are they walking through? This could be literal or metaphorical.

In Laura's second verse, she describes the moon as a sister that lights the way through the darkness. Choose an element of nature (or perhaps a material object) that will represent hope to the person you are thinking of and make them feel less alone.

ACKNOWLEDGEMENTS

'menagerie' was first published in *Nightingale & Sparrow*, 2023.

'bad fairytale' was first published in *Fireflies and Flames*, 2022.

'winter spell' was first published in *Frozen Wavelets*, 2021.

'sapling' was first published in *briefly write*, 2022.

'gift note' and 'the solitude of guarding a dragon' were first published in *L'Audacia*, 2025.

'come in & meet the cat' was first published in *Northern Gravy*, 2024.

'my sister dreams she is a garden' was a finalist for the *Dylan Thomas Day Prize*, 2023.

'my sister dreams she is a garden' and 'Five Clues For Working Out Which Bird You've Become' were first published in *The High Window*, 2025.

'Disappointing Ducks' and 'Refusal' were first published in *Atrium*, 2025.

'I complain to my friend who has been turned into a tree' was first published in *The Irish Times* and on The Caterpillar Poetry Prize website, 2025.

THANK-YOUS

I owe a whole big cauldron full of gratitude to many magical friends who helped me with this book:

Thank you my dear, supportive family & familiars!

Darling sisters, niblings, dragon-sitters, spell-singers, charm-casters, conjurers, tree-savers, wise women, loved ones, seers, diviners, magical helpers, you all know who you are!

Thank you dear poets who have taught and enchanted me!

Thank you Emma & everyone at The Emma Press for making my dream come true! Thank you Georgia and the wonderful Ark Kings Academy Marketing Team!

Thank you Kate for the fabulous artwork – I am your biggest fan & so in awe of your talent!

Thank you Sophie, Léonie, Jennie and Jess – most of these poems only magicked themselves into existence because of our precious Friday writing nights and I am so grateful for all the inspiration, kindness and support...

Thank you Cesca, Clare, Jak and Harriet for being such an amazing and encouraging storytelling coven!

Thank you Rosie, Ditte, Anders, Claire, Aget, Ella, and all of Catweazle for singing spells with me...

Thank you Lucy, Daisy, Matt, Tom, Kiran, Jess, Pia, and ALL the Sams!! Thank you Phoebe, Rowena, everyone at LIT and OPL for making poetry magic happen around me!

Thank you Nick, for putting up with all my witchy ways, on the good and bad days...

And thank you, dearest reader holding this book, for the most powerful magic of all!

ABOUT THE AUTHOR

Laura Theis grew up in a place where each street was named after a different fairy tale. She writes in her second language. Her work has appeared in *POETRY, Oxford Poetry, Magma, Rattle, Mslexia, The Caterpillar, Tyger Tyger*, and others. She received the Alpine Fellowship Writing Prize, the Oxford Brookes Poetry Prize, the Poets & Players Prize, the Hammond House International Literary Award, the AM Heath Prize, the Mogford Short Story Prize, as well as a Forward Prize nomination. Her poetry debut was the winner of the Brian Dempsey Memorial Prize, an Oxford Poetry Library Book-of-the-Month, and an Elgin Award nominee. Her collection *A Spotter's Guide To Invisible Things* won the Live Canon Collection Prize and received the Arthur Welton Award from the Society of Authors. Her most recent collection is *Introduction To Cloud Care* (Broken Sleep Books).

ABOUT THE ILLUSTRATOR

Kate Lucy Foster creates illustrations that are 'natural, cosy and textural'. She is inspired by the world around her and loves to incorporate nature into her work. She combines traditional printmaking, sketching, painting and digital work to give her illustrations an authentic, hand-made quality. Kate studied illustration at Birmingham City University.

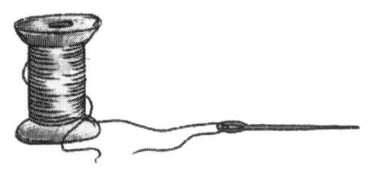

ABOUT THE EMMA PRESS

The Emma Press is an independent publishing house based in Birmingham. It was founded in 2012 by Emma Dai'an Wright and has grown to five part-time staff members following support from Arts Council England's Elevate programme in 2020-23.

The Emma Press specialises in poetry, short fiction and children's books, with translations across all genres. Recent publications have won the Michael Marks Illustration Award and been shortlisted for the CLiPPA and the Week Junior Book Awards.

In 2024 The Emma Press was a Regional Finalist for Small Press of the Year Award in the British Book Awards, as well as shortlisted for the Independent Publishers Guild's Alison Morrison Diversity, Equity & Inclusion Award.

theemmapress.com
@TheEmmaPress

ALSO FROM THE EMMA PRESS

The Skeleton in the Cupboard and other stories

Lilija Berzinska
Translated by Žanete Vēvere
Pasqualini and Sara Smith

Across nine deeply atmospheric and compelling fairytales, Lilija Berzinska follows the desires and anxieties of a community of mysterious creatures in the north of Latvia, gently exploring their preoccupations and suggesting solutions with resonant empathy and wisdom.

'An utterly charming collection and a great example of why translated literature for children is important' – Nikki Gamble, *Book Breeze Spooky Round Up*

PAPERBACK ISBN 9781915628206
PRICE £8.99

ALSO FROM THE EMMA PRESS

Eggenwise

Poems by Andrea Davidson
Illustrated by Amy Louise Evans

Can you feel homesick and at home at the same time? Ever felt lost for words but full of things to say? Meet Andrea Davidson. In *Eggenwise*, Andrea explores moving to a different country, learning a new language, growing up and falling in love through poems that notice the remarkable in the everyday: a salted parsley sprig, thundering raindrops on windowpanes, and the buzzzZZZzzz of a pesky pet fly.

Through warm and conversational verse, *Eggenwise* invites you to step into the author's new home in Belgium, to roll your tongue around new words, savour their sound and share your own story through poetry…Suitable for readers aged 10+.

PAPERBACK ISBN 9781915628091
PRICE £8.99